LEVEL
3
AGES 7 AND 8

EVEREST

RE

Joy Masoff

SCHOLASTIC
REFERENCE

PHOTO CREDITS:

Cover: Galen Rowell/Corbis; back cover: Hulton-Deutsch Collection/Corbis. Page 1:
Alfred Gregory/Royal Geographical Society; 3: Courtesy of the collection of Sarah
Longacre; 4: Hulton-Deutsch Collection/Corbis; 6 (left): Bettmann/Corbis; 6 (right):
Hulton-Deutsch Collection/Corbis; 9: Galen Rowell/Corbis; 10: AP/Wide World Photos;
11: Galen Rowell/Corbis; 12: Royal Geographical Society; 15: Hulton-Deutsch
Collection/Corbis; 18: W. Noyce/Royal Geographical Society; 21: Hulton-Deutsch
Collection/Corbis; 23: Royal Geographical Society; 24: Alfred Gregory/Royal
Geographical Society; 27: AP/Wide World Photos; 28: Courtesy of the collection of Sarah
Longacre; 30: Galen Rowell/Corbis; 31: British Information Services; 33: Hulton-Deutsch
Collection/Corbis; 34: Bettmann/Corbis; 36: Michael Lewis/Corbis; 37: Bettmann/Corbis;
38: Hulton-Deutsch Collection/Corbis; 40: AP/Wide World Photos; 41: Chris
Noble/Stone/Getty Images, Inc.; 42, 43, 44: Galen Rowell/Corbis.

Library of Congress Cataloging-in-Publication Data available.

ISBN 0-439-26707-2

Book design by Kristina Albertson and Nancy Sabato
Photo research by Sarah Longacre

10 9   06 07 08

Printed in the U.S.A.   23

First trade printing, September 2002

We are grateful to Francie Alexander, reading specialist,
and to Adele Brodkin, Ph.D., developmental psychologist,
for their contributions to the development of this series.

Our thanks also to our history consultants Maggie and John Owen,
of the American Alpine Club.

CONTENTS

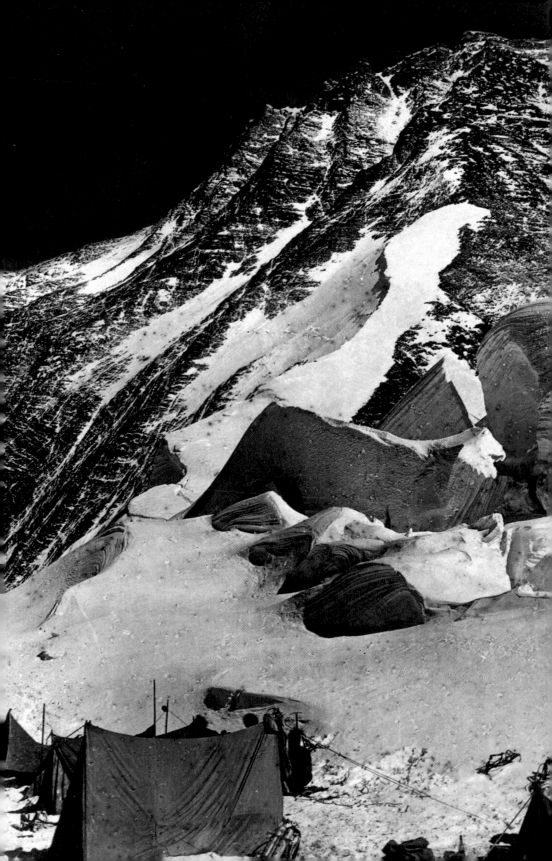

CHAPTER ONE

ALMOST THERE

It is very cold and dark outside. The sun will not rise for hours. Inside a small tent, high on the side of an ice-covered mountain, two men toss and turn. They can't sleep. All they can think of is the great adventure that lies ahead. They are about to try to do something no one has ever been able to do before. There is a good chance they might die trying.

One man is tall and thin, with a long face and wild hair. His name is Edmund Hillary. He is thirty-three years old and raises bees at home in New Zealand. This morning, he can't sleep. He crawls out of his sleeping bag, lights a small stove, and begins melting snow in a tiny pot to make drinking water. His boots have frozen solid, so he moves them closer to the stove to thaw them.

Edmund Hillary

Tenzing Norgay

The other man sits up in his sleeping bag. He is small and slim with bright eyes and a quick smile. His name is Tenzing Norgay. He is a Sherpa—a native of Nepal, a small country next to China and India. His country is home to Everest, the tallest mountain on Earth, soaring 29,035 feet (8,850 meters) above **sea level**. Here, almost 5 miles (8,046 meters) up, it is too high for birds to fly, too high for helicopters to fly. Here, just 1,200 feet (366 meters) from the top of the world's tallest mountain, it is too high for anything to survive.

Today, May 29, 1953, Hillary and Tenzing will try to climb to the top of Everest. It is a climb that will take them into a place called the **Death Zone**.

The trip to the top of Everest is full of danger. For one thing, it is bitter cold. Temperatures can drop to minus 40°F (minus 40°C). Winds can blow as hard as a hurricane with gusts up to 120 miles (193 kilometers) per hour.

THE HIMALAYAS

About 60 million years ago, the Indian subcontinent crashed into Eurasia and pushed rocks up from the seafloor. This formed a huge mountain range—the Himalayas. Amazingly, fossils of seashells have been found on many Himalayan peaks—the very highest in the world.

The ten tallest mountains on Earth are all in the Himalayas—some almost as tall as Everest. K2, on the China/Pakistan border, is only 785 feet (239 meters) shorter.

Everest was named for Sir George Everest (1790–1866), the British Surveyor General of India, who spent many years making maps of the area. Before that, the mountain was simply known as Peak XV.

Imagine about twenty Empire State Buildings on top of one another. That's how tall Everest is!

Even worse things can happen. To get to the top of the mountain, climbers must start by crossing over huge cliffs of ice called the Khumbu (**koom**-boo) **Icefall**. Hunks of ice the size

A climber jumps a crevasse on Everest.

of a house can fall and hit a person at any time. Another danger is **crevasses** (cri-**vass**-iz), which are huge ice cracks in the vast **glacier** (*glay*-shur) fields. If climbers fall in, they will fall so far their bodies will never be found.

Hillary and Tenzing, in the gear they wore when they climbed Everest.

But the greatest danger doesn't come from falling or being hit by ice. It comes from something we do every second without thinking—breathing. At this high **altitude**, there is very little oxygen in the air. The heart starts working too hard—pumping blood with not enough oxygen in it to a body starving for air. The brain then swells from too much blood and other fluid. The lungs can also fill with fluid, almost like when a person drowns.

If a person were to somehow be dropped on the top of Everest, he or she would die within one hour. How could Edmund Hillary and Tenzing Norgay hope not only to survive, but to climb up the side of the icy mountain to the **summit**, the very highest part?

The west ridge of Everest

THE DREAMERS

In their little tent, Edmund Hillary drinks some of the melted snow water and gazes up at the sky. It is growing lighter and he can see Everest's summit. Will today be the day? He dreams of how it will feel to stand at the roof of the world.

It was not enough just to dream of reaching the top of the mountain. It has taken Hillary and Tenzing almost seven weeks to climb up to this high, narrow ledge where they have spent the night. But they have been working their whole lives to reach this moment.

When he was a boy, Edmund Hillary loved to read about knights and dragons. He was terribly shy and didn't have many friends. But when he was outdoors hiking, he felt strong and brave. He could pretend that he was a hero.

Hillary's homeland, New Zealand, has lots of rugged mountains. When Edmund was sixteen years old, his school took a class trip to the mountains. He loved the brisk, clean air. But he especially loved to push his body to the limit.

Climbing was thrilling, and Edmund Hillary climbed every chance he could get. He met other climbers who taught him new skills. In time, he grew very strong, sometimes riding his bike for hours just to reach a good climbing spot.

Soon, he looked for even greater challenges.
He went off to climb in the Swiss Alps, then
moved on to the even taller Himalayas.

By the spring of 1952, Edmund Hillary
was one of the strongest climbers in the world.

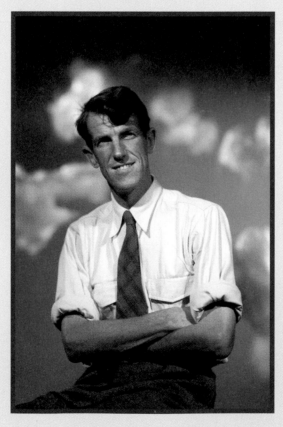

Edmund Hillary

Tenzing Norgay grew up just 20 miles (32 kilometers) from Everest. He, too, dreamed of adventure, but life was very hard where he lived. He was the eleventh of thirteen children and worked as a yak herder to help his family. When he was eighteen, he moved to India to earn a better living. He got a job as a porter, a person who carries heavy loads up mountains for climbing trips. Everyone liked him, so he got a lot of work. And he, too, grew very strong.

Climbing Everest had always been his dream, so Tenzing returned to Nepal two years later. Over the next eighteen years, he tried to reach the summit six times. He came very close, but never made it to the top.

Would he, on his seventh try, see his dream come true?

WHAT TO TAKE TO EVEREST

You can't make it to the top of a mountain like Everest without the right gear. When Hillary and Tenzing made their climb, they wore stiff, leaky boots. They used oxygen systems that often got clogged with ice and stopped working. Most modern climbers take:

1—special hard plastic climbing boots
2—down suits and layers of polar fleece undergarments
3—ice axes
4—metal teeth, called **crampons**, which strap onto boots and grab the ice
5—breathing systems that use pure oxygen, or mix oxygen with air
6—climbing ropes and climbing hardware, including anchoring devices to secure ropes, and rescue pulleys

Hillary and Tenzing have spent years learning the ways of the mountains. Now, on this bright May morning, all their hard work will be tested. The two climbers pull on their warm down suits and the oxygen tanks that will help them breathe. They think back on the trip that has brought them this far.

Tenzing Norgay and other members of the team organize their equipment.

CHAPTER THREE

THE ADVENTURE

Hillary and Tenzing have begun their trip in Kathmandu (*kat*-man-**doo**), the capital of Nepal. It has taken nearly a month just to get to that city! There are no roads and the climbers have made the trip first by ship or plane, then train, then truck, and finally on foot. Their destination after leaving Kathmandu will be Everest **Base Camp**. It is a 124-mile (200-kilometer) walk!

It takes a month to reach Everest Base Camp. The men have moved slowly uphill, beginning their journey by crossing through a steamy jungle filled with hungry tigers, crocodiles, and snakes. They wade through streams filled with blood-sucking worms, called leeches. They sway across narrow rope bridges. Temperatures get colder as they move higher.

Hillary and Tenzing have not come alone. They are part of an expedition (*ek*-spuh-**dish**-uhn)—a team of fourteen people who have come from England and New Zealand. Joining them are 30 Sherpas and 350 porters who will carry all their gear. Without these people, there can be no Everest climb.

The Sherpas and porters carry almost 22,000 pounds (9,979 kilograms) of food and equipment, including tents and warm clothing.

Most important of all are the oxygen tanks that will help the team breathe as they move higher up the mountain. Some men carry more than 60 pounds (27 kilograms) on their backs.

The Sherpas of Nepal

The Sherpas have lived in the shadow of Everest for about 500 years. They have become used to the high altitude of the region, so it doesn't affect them as much as it does others.

Today, many of these mountain people of Nepal are master climbers. Sherpas have made it to the top of Everest faster and more often than anyone else. Sadly, many have died on the mountain. The first recorded deaths on Everest happened in 1922. Seven Sherpa porters were killed in an **avalanche**.

As the team climbs higher, the climbers' bodies get used to breathing the thinner air. Their blood starts making more hemoglobin (**hee**-moh-*gloh*-bin) to carry oxygen to their hearts and lungs.

Their first stop is at 12,887 feet (3,928 meters) above sea level. They set up a rear camp so their bodies can get used to the high altitudes. After three weeks, they move on to Everest Base Camp—18,000 feet (5,486 meters) above sea level. Every day, they slowly make their way up through the dangerous Khumbu Icefall, moving their equipment up the mountain bit by bit.

Edmund Hillary loves it up here. Every day, he sets up bridges across the deep crevasses by tying ladders together.

One very scary day, he almost falls to his death. Luckily, he is roped to Tenzing who quickly stops his fall. The two become close friends after that.

John Hunt, leader of the Everest team, in his tent

For the next few weeks, the team keeps moving higher up the mountain, setting up camp at greater altitudes. Finally, they reach Camp 8—the highest camp for the team. They are almost there!

John Hunt, the team leader, picks his two strongest climbers to try to reach the top of Everest first. Edmund Hillary and Tenzing Norgay are not chosen to go.

Then disaster strikes. The oxygen tanks don't work, and the first two climbers have to turn back. Hillary and Tenzing are told that they will have a chance to reach the summit after all!

Hillary and Tenzing feel excited, yet calm, as they begin their climb to the top. After spending the night perched on their little ledge, they are ready to make the final climb. It is minus 17°F (minus 27°C), and they have pulled on eight layers of clothing and three pairs of gloves. Their backpacks weigh 40 pounds (18 kilograms) each.

The two men move slowly, carefully hacking steps into the ice with their axes. Parts of the climb are really scary—ridges that are only as wide as a diving board. There are places where the mountain falls off 2 miles (3 kilometers) straight down. One wrong step could mean death.

Still, up they go, higher and higher, until they come to a rocky wall—40 feet (12 meters) high. Now what?

Hillary sees a slim crack in the rock. He jams a foot into it and begins to wiggle up, grabbing at any handhold he can find. Tenzing follows. They haven't come this far only to give up!

It takes almost half an hour to inch up using the crack. They can barely catch their breath. What else can happen?

The two men keep going up. They move from rock to snow, and soon they can climb no more because there is no more mountain left.

They have summitted—they have reached the top! Their tiredness quickly gives way to joy as they look out at the awesome sight all around them.

Tenzing Norgay, at the summit of Everest

Postes
1998
OPG

500 GNF

1953 ~ La Conquête de l'Everest

RÉpublique de Guinée

CHAPTER FOUR

ON THE TOP

As they stand happily at Everest's summit, Hillary tries to shake Tenzing's hand, but Tenzing throws his arms around his friend and gives him a great big bear hug. Hillary takes photos to prove they are there. Tenzing leaves a gift of candies and cookies to honor the great goddess Chomolungma (cho-mah-**lung**-ma)—mother of the earth—for his people believe she lives up here.

After just fifteen minutes it is time to start down. The oxygen in their tanks is running out. Because they are tired, they must be extra careful. Going down is even harder than climbing up. Weary muscles can lead to missteps and dangerous, even deadly, falls.

Four hours later, Hillary and Tenzing slowly make their way back into Camp 8.

FLAGS FOR BUDDHA

The religion of the Sherpa people is called Buddhism (**boo**-diz-um). One of the ways they pray is by flying prayer flags—pieces of brightly colored silk or cotton that have special symbols and messages printed on them. The Sherpas believe that as the wind flutters across each flag it will carry its prayer—wishes for long life, good health, or thankfulness—to everyone. Prayer flags fly until they fall apart so that the prayers can return to the earth.

All along the steep passes that lead to Everest, brightly colored flags flutter in the breeze. Everest is indeed a holy place to the Sherpas.

Hillary is congratulated by Sherpas after going down from the summit to Camp 4.

Hillary grins and tells George Lowe, one of the other climbers, that they have left the first footprints *ever* in the snows at the summit of Everest.

There is no way to tell the rest of the expedition, waiting farther down on the mountain, the news, so the team will not learn that Hillary and Tenzing have reached the top until the next afternoon.

Right now, the two men are so very tired. They are proud of what they have done, but they don't think the rest of the world will care very much.

They are wrong!

Halfway around the world, England is about to crown a new queen. One of the first things Queen Elizabeth will do is make Edmund Hillary a Knight of the British Empire. (New Zealand was part of the British Empire.) All Hillary can think of when he hears that he will be knighted is that he has nothing to wear! He will have to get a new pair of pants, pants good enough to wear in the presence of the queen.

Tenzing Norgay holds the ice axe he used on Everest,
while Edmund Hillary stands beside him. Also in the
picture are John Hunt, and Tenzing's wife and daughter.

Hillary and Tenzing wear medals given to them by the king of Nepal.

FAME

The two climbers are superstars. Everyone treats these two quiet, modest men like heroes. Edmund Hillary is now *Sir* Edmund Hillary. Tenzing Norgay is awarded the Star of Nepal. They see their faces on postage stamps and magazine covers. Buildings are named after them.

Sir Edmund Hillary receives a warm welcome from students in a town where he has helped to bring about the construction of a school and a hospital.

However, it isn't with stamps and buildings that Hillary and Tenzing will leave their mark on the world. And reaching the top of Everest will not be their greatest accomplishment. Instead, they use their newfound fame to help the people of the Himalayas. They raise money to build hospitals and schools for the people of Nepal.

Doctors can now come to help the Sherpas. New airstrips allow planes to bring much-needed equipment. Teachers have schools to teach in.

In the end, Edmund Hillary and Tenzing Norgay have become heroes not only because of the mountain they climbed but because of the good they did after they came down.

Twenty-five years after reaching the top of Everest, Tenzing Norgay shows off some of the equipment he used.

In the years to come, the two men will go their separate ways—although they will remain lifelong friends.

Edmund Hillary never gives up dreaming of great adventures. Even at the very moment he was standing atop Everest, he was looking down at another very steep mountain, planning how he might climb it if he got the chance.

Sir Edmund Hillary

Hillary will brave the icy cold of Antarctica and drive a tractor to the South Pole. He will return to the Himalayas to search for the legendary *yeti*, also called the Abominable (uh-**bom**-in-a-*bull*) Snowman. And Hillary will almost die when he gets **altitude sickness** on a climb.

But Hillary's greatest feat will be years of hard work in Nepal, the country he has come to love, for the Sherpas, the people to whom he owes so much.

Tenzing Norgay will become a goodwill ambassador and a role model for the Sherpa people. He will start the Himalayan Mountaineering Institute, teaching and training climbers until his death in 1986.

Sir Edmund Hillary with his family, including his son Peter, who would reach the summit of Everest as an adult.

The great mountain, Everest, will still call out to climbers all over the world. Many will follow in Hillary's and Tenzing's footsteps. Two who will reach the summit are Peter, Edmund Hillary's son, and Jamling, Tenzing Norgay's son. Tenzing's grandson Tashi will also reach the summit forty-four years after his grandfather's famous climb.

Others will leave
their own marks in the
snows of Everest.
Climbers will reach the
top by blazing new,
more difficult trails.

An Italian climber
named Reinhold
Messner reached the
summit without using any bottled oxygen in
1978, then made a solo climb, again with no
oxygen, in 1980. In 2001, a sixteen-year-old,
Temba Tsheri Sherpa, who had lost several
fingers to frostbite in an earlier attempt,
became the youngest to reach the top of
Everest. Also in 2001, a blind American
named Erik Weihenmayer proudly stood at
the roof of the world—an awesome feat.

In time, some people will begin to take the mighty mountain for granted. But on Everest, high up in the Death Zone, danger still remains. Brutal storms still creep up and kill

Ice climbing on Everest

without warning. The deep, snow-covered crevasses are always deadly traps. Almost 200 men and women have died on the slopes of Everest.

As more and more people come to climb Everest, there are human traffic jams on the summit, since there are only a few days in the year when the weather will allow a climb to the top.

Climbers leave their empty oxygen bottles in the snow as they climb. After almost eighty years, there are thousands of empty bottles littering the mountain. Old ripped tents and abandoned gear have left the mountain looking like a trash heap.

Somehow, Everest must be returned to the way it looked—unspoiled and very beautiful—when Hillary and Tenzing first set out to "knock off the mountain."

Yaks carry supplies to a camp at the base of Everest.

EARTY WELCOME TO SIR EDMUND HILLARY AND OTHER MEMBERS FOR THE
APPY REUNION IN NEPAL ON THE OCCASION OF THE 40ᵗʰ ANNIVERSARY
= THE HISTORICAL CONQUEST OF MOUNT EVEREST IN 1953.

SHERPA RECEPTION COMMITTEE

Sir Edmund Hillary and other members of the expedition, including Sir John Hunt, attended a reunion in Kathmandu, to celebrate the fortieth anniversary of the conquest of Everest.

The snowy footprints that Edmund Hillary and Tenzing Norgay left on the summit of Everest have long since vanished. But their achievement of pushing themselves to their limits and doing the impossible still stands—as towering as the mountain that inspired them.

CHRONOLOGY

1856   A survey of India finds that Peak XV in the Himalayas is the world's tallest mountain.

1865   Peak XV is named Everest after Sir George Everest, the British Surveyor General.

1922   The first attempt to climb Everest is made by a British team including George Mallory, the famous mountaineer.

1924   George Mallory and Andrew Irvine disappear as they attempt to reach the summit of Everest. Some believe they may have made it to the top, only to perish on the way down.

1953   Hillary and Tenzing reach the top of Everest.

1955   Everest is proven to be 26 feet (8 meters) taller than the original measurements of the 1856 survey.

1963   James Whittaker becomes the first American to summit Everest.

1975   A Japanese woman, Junko Tabei, becomes the first female to reach the top of Everest.

1980   Italian climber Reinhold Messner makes a solo climb without bottled oxygen.

1996   Storms claim the lives of fifteen climbers—the most deaths in a single year.

1999   George Mallory's frozen body is finally found, at 27,000 feet (8,230 meters). And a new height is determined for Everest— 29,035 feet (8,850 meters).

2001   Temba Tsheri Sherpa, sixteen, becomes the youngest ever to summit Everest.

GLOSSARY

altitude—height above sea level

altitude sickness—swelling of the brain from lack of oxygen at very high altitudes

avalanche—a mass of snow, rock, and ice that suddenly and swiftly sweeps down a mountain, destroying everything in its path

base camp—a central place where climbers store tents, food, and medical equipment

crampons—metal frames with spikes that are strapped on over hiking boots to grab into the ice

crevasses (cri-**vass**-iz)—deep open gaps in a glacier

Death Zone—altitudes above 27,000 feet (8,230 meters) where there is only one-third of the oxygen found at sea level

glacier (**glay**-shur)—a large mass of slowly creeping ice and snow formed in places where more snow falls than can melt

icefall—cascades of ice that form when glaciers hit hills and ridges

sea level—the level of the waters of Earth's seas at the point between high and low tide

summit—the highest point on a mountain

INDEX

NOTE TO PARENTS

A whole world of discovery opens for children once they begin to read. Illustrated stories and chapter books are wonderful fun for children, but it is just as important to introduce your son or daughter to the world of nonfiction. The ability to read and comprehend factual material is essential for all children, both in school and throughout life.

History is full of fascinating people and places. Scholastic History Readers™ feature clear texts and wonderful photographs of real-life adventures from days gone by.

FOR FURTHER READING

COBURN, BROUGHTON.
Triumph on Everest: A Photobiography of Sir Edmund Hillary.
Washington, D.C.: National Geographic Society, 2000.

STEWART, WHITNEY.
Sir Edmund Hillary: To Everest and Beyond.
Minneapolis: Lerner Publications Company, 1996.